Legend of the Li River

An Ancient Chinese Tale
Retold and Illustrated by
Jeanne M. Lee

Holt, Rinehart and Winston
New York

To my father and mother

Copyright © 1983 by Jeanne M. Lee
All rights reserved, including the right to reproduce
this book or portions thereof in any form.
Published by Holt, Rinehart and Winston,
383 Madison Avenue, New York, New York 10017.
Published simultaneously in Canada by Holt, Rinehart
and Winston of Canada, Limited.
First Edition

Printed in the United States of America
10 9 8 7 6 5 4 3 2 1

Library of Congress Cataloging in Publication Data

Lee, Jeanne M.
  Legend of the Li River.
  Summary: A sea princess who wishes to lessen the
hardships of the poor laborers employed in building the
Great Wall of China seeks help from the Goddess of Mercy.
  [1. Folklore—China.   2. Great Wall of China (China)—
Fiction.]   I. Title.
PZ8.1.L367Ld   1983   398.2'1'0951   [E]   83-79
ISBN 0-03-063523-3

The author wishes to thank Mimi B. Soloman
for her invaluable advice.

ISBN 0-03-063523-3

The Li River flows through southeastern China. Its crystal waters gleam amidst the magical hills of its banks. This legend tells how the beauty of this river came into being.

More than two thousand years ago, when China
first became an empire, its mighty Emperor was
anxious to guard his land from northern invaders.
He ordered the building of the Great Wall
across the northern boundary of China.

Earth and stones had to be transported from
far away to build the huge wall. Thousands of
men were forced by soldiers to carry the
heavy materials to the building site.

In the summer, these men carried loads of earth and small stones on their bare backs.

In the winter, they flooded
the roads with water and were
able to glide the larger stones
over the ice. Still, these men endured
great hardships and many of them died.

Deep in the South China Sea, the young daughter
of the Dragon King had been watching the men
from her window. The little princess wept
as she watched the suffering of the poor
stone carriers.

The little princess decided to seek help
from the Goddess of Mercy.

The Goddess offered this solution: "If we move the rocks of the South Sea to the north, we will save these men much suffering. This willow twig will move the rocks for you. But you must promise not to speak to anyone on your path, or the magic of the willow twig will disappear."

After the little princess made the promise, she took the twig and thanked the Goddess of Mercy for her help.

Back in the deep blue sea, the princess
swayed the willow twig gently in the water.
The rocks in the bottom of the sea stirred
as if awakened.

Tigers, oxen, camels, horses,
and elephants emerged
from the deep blue sea.

The animals then swam toward shore.
Amazed, the little princess
quickly picked up the magic twig
and followed the animals.
She herded them together
on the beach and pointed
the twig north.

At first the animals walked slowly.

Then they started to run as if in a hurry. With her willow twig in hand, the little princess kept close behind. For days and nights they ran north.

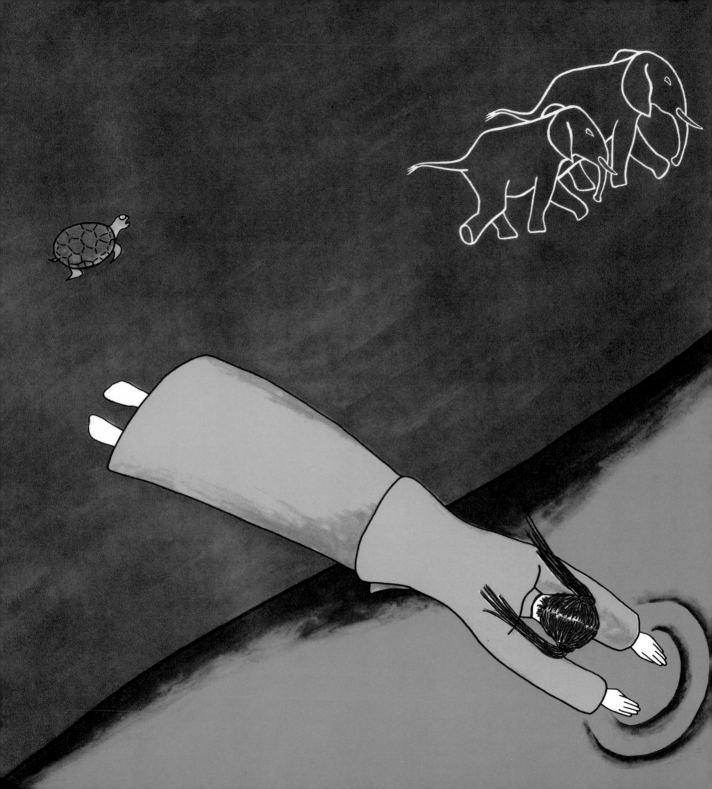

The princess of the sea became quite thirsty
and tired as she ran inland for such a
long time. When she came to a gleaming river,
she jumped into the water for relief.

But out of the corner
of her eye, she saw the
animals moving up river
with great speed.
They were becoming
smaller and smaller.

Quickly she left the water and started
running after the animals. On the other side
of the river, an old man was strolling.
In her haste, the princess called out to him:
"Old man! Stop those animals behind you!"

Suddenly, there was great calm.
The little princess had spoken.
The animals and the old man
had disappeared. Instead, there
were only hills of rocks
along the riverbank.

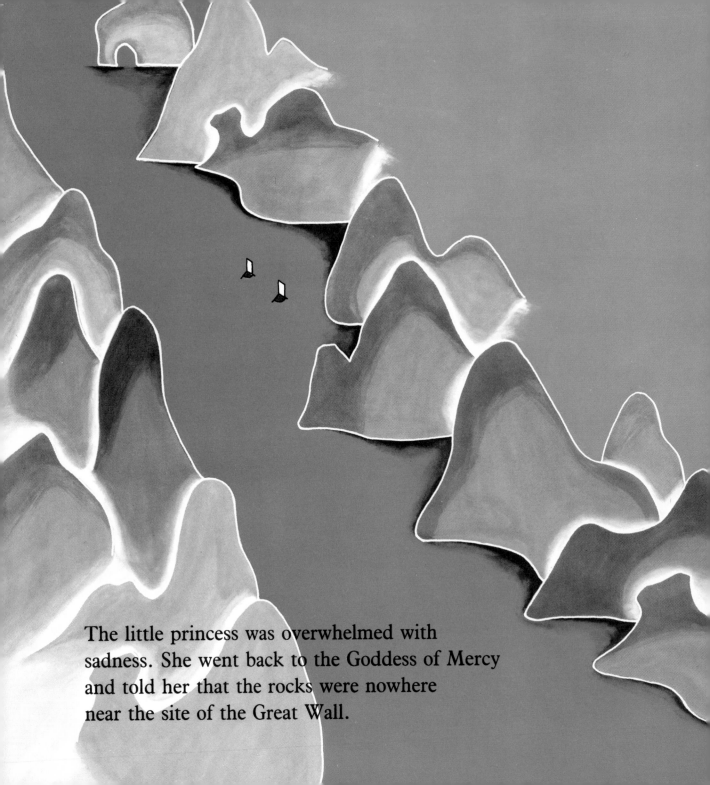

The little princess was overwhelmed with
sadness. She went back to the Goddess of Mercy
and told her that the rocks were nowhere
near the site of the Great Wall.

The kind Goddess said to her: "Do not be sad,
little princess of the sea; the rocks that
you have put along the Li River have made
it beautiful. Now poor people will have a
place to rest after their hard work.
You should be proud that you put the
rocky hills there for them."

The River winds like
   silk ribbon,
The hills rise like
   jade hairpins.

Han Yu
Tang Dynasty poet

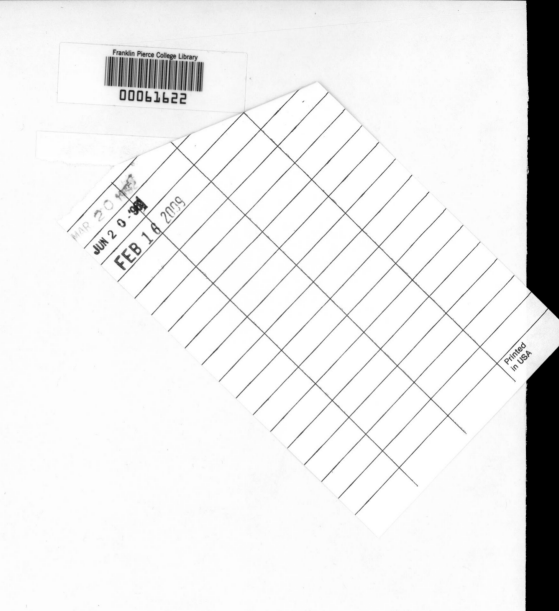